About The Bank Street Ready-to-Read Series

Seventy years of educational research and innovative teaching have given the Bank Street College of Education the reputation as America's most trusted name in early childhood education.

Because no two children are exactly alike in their development, we have designed the *Bank Street Ready-to-Read* series in three levels to accommodate the individual stages of reading readiness of children ages four through eight.

- *Level 1:* GETTING READY TO READ—read-alouds for children who are taking their first steps toward reading.
- *Level 2:* READING TOGETHER—for children who are just beginning to read by themselves but may need a little help.
- *Level 3:* I CAN READ IT MYSELF—for children who can read independently.

Our three levels make it easy to select the books most appropriate for a child's development and enable him or her to grow with the series step by step. The *Bank Street Ready-to-Read* books also overlap and reinforce each other, further encouraging the reading process.

We feel that making reading fun and enjoyable is the single most important thing that you can do to help children become good readers. And we hope you'll be a part of Bank Street's long tradition of learning through sharing.

The Bank Street College of Education

ANNIE'S PET

A Bantam Little Rooster Book
Simultaneous paper-over-board and trade paper editions/July 1989

Little Rooster is a trademark of Bantam Books,
a division of Bantam Doubleday Dell Publishing Group, Inc.

Series graphic design by Alex Jay/Studio J
Associate Editor: Randall Reich

Special thanks to James A. Levine, Betsy Gould,
Erin B. Gathrid, and Herb Valen.

Library of Congress Cataloging-in-Publication Data

Brenner, Barbara.
Annie's pet.

(Bank Street ready-to-read)
"A Byron Preiss book."
"A Bantam little rooster book."
Summary: On her way to the pet shop to buy an animal with her birthday money, Annie buys a toy, a collar, a dish, and a leash and discovers that she has no money left for a pet.
[1. Pets—Fiction] I. Ziegler, Jack, ill.
II. Title. III. Series.
PZ7.B7518An 1989 [E] 88-7965
ISBN 0-553-05833-9
ISBN 0-553-34693-8 (pbk.)

Published simultaneously in the United States and Canada

Bantam Books are published by Bantam Books, a division of Bantam Doubleday Dell Publishing Group, Inc. Its trademark, consisting of the words "Bantam Books" and the portrayal of a rooster, is Registered in U.S. Patent and Trademark Office and in other countries. Marca Registrada. Bantam Books, 666 Fifth Avenue, New York, New York 10103.

PRINTED IN THE UNITED STATES OF AMERICA

WAK 0 9 8 7 6 5 4

Bank Street Ready-to-Read™

by Barbara Brenner
Illustrated by Jack Ziegler

A Byron Preiss Book

A BANTAM LITTLE ROOSTER BOOK
NEW YORK · TORONTO · LONDON · SYDNEY · AUCKLAND

On her birthday, Annie went to the zoo. That's where she got a great idea.

"I have five birthday dollars,"
she said to her family.
"I'm going to buy an animal."

Annie didn't know
what kind of animal she wanted.
But she knew
what kind she didn't want.

"I don't want a bear," she said.
"Bears are too hairy."

"I don't want a snake.
You can't take a snake for a walk."

"Try not to buy too big an animal," said her father.

"You don't want too small an animal," said her mother.

"Get a wild animal," said her brother.
"I don't want a wild animal," said Annie.
"I want a *pet*."

The next day, Annie put on her hat and her backpack.
"So long, everybody," she said.
"I'm going to buy my pet."

Annie walked down the street
until she came to a house.
There was a girl with a bird
in front of the house.

The bird gave Annie an idea.

Annie called to the girl,
"Will you sell that bird
for five dollars?"
"Not for a million dollars.
I love this bird."

"But I need a pet to love, too,"
said Annie.
"Try the pet store," said the girl.
And she went inside with her bird.

Annie walked a little more.
She came to a toy store.
The store gave her an idea.

"Do you have toys for pets?"
she asked the man inside.
"All kinds," said the man.
"Swings, rings, bells, balls."

"I'll take a ball."
"That will be one dollar,"
said the man.
Annie gave the man one dollar.
She still had four dollars.

Annie walked a little more.
She came to a gift shop.
A pretty tan cat was sitting
in the window.

Annie went into the shop.
"How much is that cat in the window?"
she asked the woman.
"That cat is not for sale,"
said the woman.
"We do not sell pets.
But we do sell pet collars."

"Now that's a great idea," said Annie. "A collar—not too big, not too small."

Annie bought a collar for one dollar. She still had three dollars.

Annie walked a little more.
She went into a store
in a shopping mall.
She saw a nice red pet dish
and a nice red pet leash.
They each cost one dollar.
Annie bought the dish and the leash.

“Now I have all the things
I’ll need for my pet,” she said.

Annie’s long walk had
made her very hungry.
So she stopped to buy a little snack.
It only cost one dollar.

At last, Annie came to the pet store.
She looked in the window.
There were pets of every size and kind.

“This is it,” cried Annie.
“This is where I’ll buy my pet.”

Annie reached into the backpack
to get her money.
But the money was gone!

She thought about what
she had spent—
one dollar for a toy . . .
one dollar for a collar . . .
one dollar for a dish . . .
one dollar for a leash . . .
and one dollar for a double-dip cone!
Five—Annie had spent
all five birthday dollars!

Annie sat down on a stone step
to have a good cry.
But then she looked up
and saw a sign that read:

That's when Annie got
the greatest idea of all!
She jumped up and ran inside.

"I'm looking for a pet," said Annie.
"Can you give a pet a good home?"
asked the woman behind the desk.
"Yes," said Annie.
"I have a collar, a toy, a dish,
and a leash for my pet.
But I don't have any money."

“Do you have love?” asked the woman.
“Oh, yes, I have a lot of that,” said Annie.
“Then I have just the pet for you,”
the woman said.

And she did.